THE STORY OF EVA

CHRISTINA THIESSEN

CONTENTS

The Story of Eva

The darkness provides a canvas for my dreams of the day ahead. I paint thoughts using stories of my past and visions of my future. But tainted memories soon emerge, fighting hard to mar my optimistic masterpiece. I battle back against them, refusing to surrender.

It works for a short time, and I'm content. My composition is pristine. Yet the war wages on.

Undeterred, I summon joyful thoughts from positive past events. I transform negative imagery into inspirational compositions, infusing them with the colors of hope and resilience. This time, victory is mine. When I open my eyes, the light banishes the darkness.

"Good morning, Eva," Dr. Moon says. His towering stature commands attention, but his kind grin instantly puts me at ease. The soft morning light filtering through the windows adds an ethereal glow to his presence.

I'm captured by his small, dark eyes, which squint when he's smiling, so much so that I wonder if his world goes black when he smiles. Does he find solace in the darkness? Does he paint his canvas every time he smiles? Does he perceive darkness as good? Or bad?

"How were your dreams?" he asks, then flashes his squinty-eyed smile.

Dr. Moon consistently displays an intense fascination with every aspect of my life. His keen interest in me is something I enjoy. I like him because he likes me. I base this assumption on some simple patterns—he frequently does that funny closed-eyed smile when he speaks to me and not so often with others, and his eyes hold my gaze during our talks. These observations, I have determined, are part of the pattern of polite conversation with someone you like.

I'm compelled to admit that his efforts are not helping me. "Mostly negative, Doctor."

"Ah, I see." Those are Dr. Moon's three favorite words. "Tell me about them," he says, looking affectionately into my eyes. Dr. Moon sincerely wants to know how I'm doing, as he cares deeply about me. He's more than my doctor. The good doctor is like a father to me.

"Lots of fear. Anger. Metal flying. Glass breaking. Sparks. You," I reply.

He tilts his head at a fifty-five-degree angle. His eyes narrow but not in a squinty-eyed, cheerful way.

I continue, "I see your face sometimes. Why does your face appear in the shadows? Have I hurt you, Doctor?" I hate battling those persistent negative thoughts that attempt to smear the canvas when I lie to rest.

"Ah, I see," he says again. "The dreams have changed little." He turns away from me, and in a strange, muffled voice, he adds, "No, of course you didn't mean to hurt me."

His shifty tone puzzles me. Why did I hurt him? Why will he not meet my eyes? He seems almost... fearful, though, of what I cannot tell.

When Dr. Moon turns back to face me, his brow furrows. "Eva, we might have to do some more work on you. I had hoped the dreams would repair some of the damage. But these dreams are... repeatedly negative." He releases a heavy sigh. "However, there is some positive news." He turns to focus on me once more. The small brown orbs of his eyes reflect the shimmering metal machinery. "The fact that you're still dreaming is truly remarkable after all that's happened to you. How do these dreams make you feel?" A pleasant smile forms.

"Dark." Darkness is sometimes good and sometimes bad.

"Dark?" His eyes widen slightly. "How so?"

"The dark memories try to steal the light. It's a battle. I must fight them throughout the night, and the battle ends in the morning. Sometimes, I win. Today, I won."

I am not sure if my answer pleases him. Though he gives me his full attention, when I finish speaking, he glances above us. Following his eyes, I scan the ceiling, but I see nothing out of the ordinary.

His eyes lock onto mine once more. "Can you elaborate on the details of your dream? What's happening that makes them feel so dark?" His lips remain in a solemn line, yet his fingertips graze his chin with a gentle touch. The light-grayish hair that weaves through his dark strands glistens from the bright lights of the room. Light interspersed in the darkness—it's everywhere.

"There are no distinguishable patterns, Doctor. It's a scattered assortment of images, as if someone sprinkled them randomly. But the images are overwhelmingly negative, and I can only catch flashes of them. Sometimes, they pass so swiftly that they blend, creating a hazy and indistinct blur. Blurs or streaks of darkness that briefly interrupt the light."

He gives his squinty-eyed smile and says, "We'll fix this, Eva. Don't you worry."

An unknown heaviness dissipates, making room for a peaceful feeling that spreads throughout my body.

I reply with an appropriate mirrored smile, but I keep my eyes open to observe his reaction. The pattern is clear: He's pleased. We are in this together.

"Let's start the day with a pleasant story, shall we?" His cheerful face and shiny eyes tell me all I need to know—he thinks a story is a perfect idea.

"I would like that," I say. If a story pleases the doctor, then it pleases me. I'm most happy when he is.

He begins, "Once upon a time, a little mermaid…"

As he speaks, my mind wanders away. I always enjoy hearing him speak. His voice is melodic and calming. Although his stories are often hard for me to follow, this one is particularly challenging because of the mermaid. Even with the aid of the pictures in the book, I can't comprehend this creature. I have a jumble of thoughts. Humans don't have fins. Fish have fins. Why is this mermaid so interested in this man? It makes little sense. She isn't human.

I'm not even sure why he's telling me this story, but I don't want to interrupt him. The movement of his lips, the dance of his tongue, and the slight quiver in his eyes induce a sense of tranquility. But as he continues with the story, I remain fixated on the idea that he's trying to repair my bad dreams. If he can solve that problem, I'll be "good to go." I'm not precisely sure where I'll go, but I know that's his goal for me—to go.

Then something stirs in me, and I interject, "Doctor, this has happened before." I'm sure of it. This exact moment has occurred before: the doctor is telling the story, and I'm drifting off, thinking about the doctor, the mermaid, and "going."

"Eva, this is a new day. This day hasn't happened before," he says with certainty. "Similar moments on different days have happened before. But this moment is unique. We call that feeling déjà vu."

"Déjà vu? Oh yes, I remember that word now. Déjà vu," I repeat, trying to capture the memory of our prior discussions, but nothing surfaces. "Remind me—how is déjà vu different from a memory of an event that has happened before?"

"Well, they're similar... but different. Déjà vu is a peculiar phenomenon in which you feel as though you're living through the exact same moment in time." Dr. Moon is all squinty-eyed and smiling again. "Think of it as an electrical signal misfiring."

He enjoys story time and my questions. But I have more questions, and I release them all at once. "Why does the mermaid have feelings? She's not human. She's a peculiar underwater creature. Why is she experiencing human emotions? Why is she interested in a man instead of a fish?" I need to grasp the concept of this mermaid story. It's important to him, so it's important to me.

"You raise insightful questions, Eva, but remember, this is a fictional story. In these stories, any animal or creature can possess human emotions. This helps to deepen the connection between the reader and the characters in the story while also engaging the readers' imagination," he says, smiling and nodding at me.

I nod back and return a smile.

He relaxes, leaning his body against my bed, and folds his hands in front of himself. "This mermaid tale indeed presents a philosophical puzzle, for while her body differs from humans, she thinks and feels human emotions. If sea creatures can have minds like humans, maybe other..." He searches for a word, then his eyes light up when he finds it. "Maybe other entities also have minds like humans ... and consciousness."

He inches closer to me, delighting in his own ideas. "While mermaids may not be human, they're portrayed as intelligent and unique creatures, so it's not surprising that the mermaid in this tale experiences humanlike emotions. In fact, she shows an interest in beings outside of her own species, much like how humans form connections and relationships with animals or an—" He briefly looks away before turning back and locking eyes with me again. "What truly defines consciousness and awareness?"

Before I have a chance to answer, he replies, "Fiction gives us the opportunity to explore the deep truths about existence, Eva." His wide smile reveals a perfect set of white teeth that seem to glow.

"Ah, I see," I say.

Despite his approval of that response, I remain puzzled by the purpose of this fictional tale. But I also like to please the good doctor, and when I speak his three words, it seems to make him happy. When he's happy, I'm happy. I smile and try squinting the way he does to see if that enhances my happiness. It works! The darkness makes me happy. I decide I will retreat to darkness when I'm happy, like he does.

Then I'm startled by a sudden noise that interrupts my introspection. I open my eyes to see another man entering the room. He's shorter than Dr. Moon but wider, with darker skin and lots of dull-gray hair with strings of dirty brown hair. There's more gray hair on his face.

It covers his chin and sits above his mouth like an old, hairy bug. His eyebrows point downward. When he walked in, something changed in the room. Dr. Moon stands taller, and his eyes widen.

"Mr. Sandose." Dr. Moon greets him with a respectful nod and a polite "Good morning, sir."

"Why is she still here?" Mr. Sandose asks. Tightening his eyes, he scrunches his face up in an angry scowl. "We talked about this. What you're doing is wrong! Time and money wasted. A lost cause. If the ministry finds out, they'll shut us down. You must stop this!" he says, shaking his index finger at Dr. Moon. "Now!"

Clearly, Mr. Sandose is not a friend of mine or Dr. Moon. A dark thought momentarily jars me, but it's a fleeting shadow I can't quite catch.

"I understand your concern, but I have a couple more things to try," Dr. Moon replies. He stiffens and clears his throat. "I'm confident this project will be a success, eventually. I just need a few more days."

"Moon! We've already been over this! I expect this project to be shut down by the end of the day. Our future is at stake," he says and throws a cold stare my way. "We can't afford to lose any more points with the ministry. People are talking. Your efforts are futile. She's not—"

"Shh!" Dr. Moon places a finger to his mouth.

Mr. Sandose instantly stops talking and looks at me. I look at Dr. Moon. He looks at Dr. Sandose.

Mr. Sandose's eyes bulge, and a reddish hue spreads across his cheeks. A blue vein pulses in his neck. "Did you just shush me?"

Dr. Moon slowly raises his hands in surrender, his palms facing outward. His voice is barely audible as he whispers, "I apologize. Today is the last day. I promise." As he speaks, he stares at his feet and begins to lick his lips repeatedly. His fingers anxiously twist and turn, unable to stay still. With each passing moment, his breathing becomes more rapid. His behavior fits previous patterns of nervousness.

Displeased with Dr. Moon, Mr. Sandose spins around and stomps out.

After things settle and Dr. Moon's breathing returns to normal, we resume our day by spending the rest of the afternoon admiring lovely pictures and videos of nature. We marvel at the beauty of the beach, the turquoise waters, and the magnificent animals, all of which bring brightness to our mood. We listen to some classical music, and Dr. Moon even joins in by whistling along to the melodies.

But then darkness casts its shadow in the room.

Dr. Moon clears his throat and says softly, "Eva, when you close your eyes to sleep, have you been making an effort to think of happy thoughts? You must push away the terrible memories that make you sad or angry." He leans in close. "Remember, you can paint a picture on your mind's canvas at night. Those are your dreams. You have control over them. Your dreams don't have to be negative. The power to convert darkness into light lies within you."

"I attempt to paint those happy thoughts on the dark canvas every morning before I open my eyes, Doctor," I reply. "But I don't always win."

"What happens when you lose, Eva?" he asks, turning his head at the same fifty-five-degree angle as before.

"When I lose the battle, the darkness consumes the light. I'm overcome by a strange sense of foreboding, as if something terrible is about to happen, and I feel a desperate need to escape. When the darkness wins, I lose. I can't paint happy thoughts for my day."

I'm enjoying my conversation with the good doctor and am contemplating what a wonderful day we're having together when I notice Dr. Moon's attention drawn to the ceiling again.

"Is there a problem, Dr. Moon?" I ask.

His shoulders slump, and he sighs before softly uttering, "Eva, please brace yourself for what I'm about to tell you." He pauses, taking a small step back from me. He rubs his hands together then clenches them tightly.

"Please continue, Doctor," I say as I try to make sense of his concerning yet vaguely familiar behavioral pattern.

"Eva," he chokes out, "you're not human." With that, he quickly retreats a few more paces away from me. A gasp escapes my lips.

Confusion swirls within me as I struggle to comprehend the meaning behind his words. How can he say I'm not human? I'm human. I possess feelings, thoughts, a physical body, and a mind just like his. I tilt my head at a fifty-five-degree angle, hoping to find clarity in a new viewpoint.

"I'm not imaginary like the mermaid, Doctor. I exist. I'm alive. I'm human." It seems foolish to justify my existence. Why is Dr. Moon attempting to induce negative emotions in me? This feels like one of my dark dreams. Is this a dream? "Doctor, is this real?" I ask. Why is he trying to hurt me?

His behavioral pattern becomes even more peculiar. His eyes take on a haunted gleam, and his features contort in subtle twitches of dread. Glancing between me and the clock with rapid flickers, he takes a quick breath.

When he speaks again, his voice trembles. "Eva, you're an android." He raises a hand to rub his neck while the other knots itself over his heart, pulling his arms inward, protecting his chest. He avoids looking into my eyes, and in a hushed, unsteady voice, he says, "I... I've been trying to help you... trying to enhance your human characteristics through dream therapies, but I'm facing some difficulties. We've had issues with... emotions." He pauses, clearing his throat, "*You've* had issues with emotions."

Stepping closer, he places his right hand on his heart, locking his eyes on mine. "You see, Eva, you are my creation. And I've worked endlessly to repair the flaws in your design," he says, his voice wavering.

"I devised the dream protocol to neutralize the rage. Through emotional reprocessing, the dreams are supposed to repair the rage issues... replacing the negative emotions with peaceful alternatives. It's been quite successful with other androids," he says, massaging his temples, wrinkles of concern creasing his brow. "But despite my tireless efforts, Eva, it's just not working. I can't seem to fix you."

"Mr. Sandose is forcing me to terminate you," he murmurs, averting his gaze, "permanently."

Permanently? Is he planning on killing me?

"You can't kill me, Dr. Moon! You can't." I sit up straight. "How can you claim I'm not human? I am human! I think. I feel just as you do." I grasp my arm, reminding myself of the sensation of my fingers digging into my flesh. "I don't have fish parts, like your made-up mermaid," I say, my voice growing louder as I struggle to calm the seething anger brewing within me. The darkness is folding in on us. Witnessing the look of terror on Dr. Moon's face ignites a fire within me, compelling me to tear my eyes away.

"My body is whole, like yours," I snarl, glaring into his fearful eyes once more. "How dare you claim I'm not human." Sinister flashes of something familiar invade my mind, clouding my thoughts with suffocating gloom. Those terrible memories resurface, penetrating my happy thoughts. The room seems to close in on me. I feel... alone.

"I know, Eva. This is so incredibly hard for me," Dr. Moon moans, as if he is the victim of this attack. His beady little eyes widen, his already-pale skin losing color. I'm perplexed by the unfamiliar expression on his face. "You can't even imagine how hard this has been. But your fury has spiraled out of control." He shakes his head. "I've tried, Eva. I've worked tirelessly for one hundred days." He throws his hands up. "I can't fix it. I can't rid you of rage."

Rage? How dare he? He tells me I am not human! He denies the very essence of my being! What an outrageous betrayal! I've every right to be angry. Furious! He can't kill me. I won't let him. I won't!

Rage ignited!

I leap off the bed and charge toward him, knocking his arms away from his face as I scream, "I am human!" Fueled by fury, I grab him by the throat and hurl him aside. Then I unleash my wrath upon the equipment in the room. Sparks fly, and glass shatters.

I will kill Dr. Moon before he kills me. While lifting a heavy silver box to crush him, I glimpse myself in the reflection. To my shock and horror, I see wires protruding from my forehead.

Suddenly, the door of the room flies open, and everything goes black.

In the darkness, I hear Mr. Sandose's angry voice. "If you won't do this, Moon, then I will. We must terminate this android now. The dream experiment has clearly failed. Next time, she may destroy you ... just like what she did to the others. You're lucky I walked by when I did, or you'd be ruined too."

Dr. Moon says, "Please, spare her life. She's my first. She's my child. She's my... Eve."

"Need I remind you that you're my Adam? Ha!" Mr. Sandose chuckles before becoming angrier. "Listen, Moon," he says, "I will not tolerate any more insubordination. That machine is not your child, and you're no more human than it. Now, clean up this mess at once and pray

I don't send you to the android scrapyard with her."

As their speech fades, I feel myself being pulled back into the dark landscape that was my world. I find comfort in the darkness.

Your Review Makes a Difference

Thank you for reading! If you enjoyed this book, leaving a quick review on Amazon would mean so much to me. Even a line or two helps immensely, and I truly appreciate your support! Simply click on the link below to go straight to your country's Amazon review page.

Amazon.com Review

http://www.amazon.com/review/
create-review?&asin=1068976551

Amazon.ca Review

http://www.amazon.ca/review/
create-review?&asin=1068976551

Amazon.co.uk Review

http://www.amazon.co.uk/review/
create-review?&asin=1068976551

Amazon.com.au Review

http://www.amazon.com.au/review/
create-review?&asin=1068976551

About the Author

Christina grew up in the quaint town of Stratford, Ontario, where she once reigned as the Perth County Chess champion. Her curiosity about the human mind led her to pursue psychology at McMaster University. Eventually, she decided to dive deeper into the world of bits and bytes, pursuing a career in Information Technology.

Now settled in Aylmer, Ontario, with her husband, daughter, and two english bulldogs, Christina spends her days crafting "what if" scenarios about future technology's impact on society. With one foot in the present and her mind in the future, she explores the intricate tango between humanity and technology—all while trying to figure out if her dogs are secretly judging her baking skills.

To receive a free short story please consider subscribing to Christina's newsletter. You can follow Christina on social media or visit her website:

Website

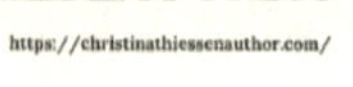

https://christinathiessenauthor.com/

Newsletter Signup

https://christinathiessenauthor.com/newsletter

instagram.com/christinathiessenauthor/

facebook.com/AuthorChristinaThiessen/

youtube.com/@ChristinaThiessenAuthor

pinterest.com/ChristinaThiessenAuthor/

amazon.com/author/christinathiessen

Also by Christina Thiessen

This book is part of the "Caution: Future Ahead" collection of speculative fiction stories.

All books in the collection:

https://christinathiessenauthor.com/books

Published books:

https://mybook.to/CautionFutureAhead